Bounce Back From Tragedy
The Collection

By

Mira Cassidy

Edited by Kendra Applewhite (KYMWrites.com)
Book Cover by Studio-A-Design (studio-a-design.com)

Visit miracassidy.com and follow Mira on social media
Twitter @mira_cassidy.com
Instagram @miracassidy.com
Facebook @authormiracassidy.com

To contact Mira regarding public speaking engagements please send an email to miracassidy@gmail.com
Motivational Speaking Topics:
Breaking Free from Domestic Violence
Overcoming Childhood Traumatic Experiences
Breaking Toxic Cycles

This book is dedicated to everyone who has bounced back from tragedy.
Keep Pushing!

The Collection

*A*bandoned

The clock on the dashboard read 7:07 p.m. After being on the road for two hours, all Trisha could do was daydream about being back at her loft in her favorite cozy, sky blue *Live, Love, Hope* sweater, comfy pajama pants, and a warm cup of chamomile tea. One more hour left to go, and she could make that fantasy a reality.

Going home to Atlanta was never an enjoyable experience. She always felt like an outsider growing up. She was the eclectic outspoken fashion designer who managed to prove all her grey-headed family authoritarians wrong by running a successful upscale boutique, where she produced and sold her own creations. Though she was successful, the fact that she didn't side with the long rich family history of non-dreaming, unvaried individuals infuriated them. They would much rather see her become a nurse, lawyer, or college professor. Trisha was satisfied and always argued that her contribution not only benefited society, but most importantly, it made her happy.

Then, there was the topic of childbirth. She was the only granddaughter to the Dixon legacy, so it was practically a sin that she didn't want children.

Bounce Back From Tragedy

As she passed the mile marker that pointed out forty-five minutes left until Savannah, an eerie tingle danced down her spine. The faint noise from under the hood of her car grew from louder to unbearable, forcing her to pull over to the side of the highway.

"Great! Just great," she muttered as she slammed one hand on the steering wheel and tugged at her dark brown naturally loose curls. She did her best to keep her cool all weekend long, but this violation caused all her pent-up frustration to erupt, resulting in a massive flow of tears.

Trisha buried her face in her hands. In one way, she felt a sense of relief. She didn't need to wait until she got to her loft to express all the hurt, despair, and anger she felt. Yet, on the other hand, she was all alone on the side of the road on a chilled winter night. To top it off, it was starting to mist. Trisha began to ponder over the dinner table discussion she managed to escape.

***

"So, who's the man in your life you've been keeping locked away from us? You're drop dead gorgeous, so you must surely have a man you're hiding from the family." Dottie gestured with her right hand, causing all of the jewelry on her wrist to clink together. *"So, come on... spill the beans baby."*

"Aunt Dottie," Trisha said grinning with embarrassment. "I don't have a man, and I don't need one. I'm perfectly fine with it being just me."

"Honey girl, you are 28 and not getting any younger."

"And I want to see my great-grandchild from my only granddaughter before I die!" Grandma chimed in.

Trisha felt a fresh rush of adrenaline. "Really Grandma? I've said it before and I'll say it again," she said, motioning to her physique. "Trisha is not allowing anything to come up out of this." Her aunts, uncles, cousins, parents, and grandma murmured in disagreement.

Her oldest cousin Kenny leaned toward her. "Trish," he whispered still chewing a piece of tender ham. "It's okay, you can tell me. You like girls, don't you?"

"What!" She jerked her head toward him, almost giving herself whiplash.

"Alright, alright. Leave my baby alone." Her mother's commanding voice came to her rescue.

"That's what we're trying to get her to have… a baby," Trisha's grandmother replied.

"Settle down," Trisha's father chimed in. "Baby girl, what about Jason, you know from high school? Weren't you both at USC together?"

"Daddy, Jason and I were just friends."

"Now you know that you're the only granddaughter, so it's a special thing for the family to see you happy and with a family *of your own," added her uncle while wiping his finely groomed beard with a napkin.*

"Uncle Carl," she responded. "It's not like this family is low on Dixons. Look at how well all the men are producing." She pointed to the children running nearby, darting for the nearest door that would take them outside to play.

"Will you all just let her be?" Trisha's mother pleaded.

"Trisha, you know your mother and I would like to experience being grandparents by our only girl. You're a wonderful woman, and you'd make a great mother. Even if you don't want children of your own. I need to see you happy, baby. You spend so much time alone and in that boutique."

Trisha tossed a sarcastic glance toward her father and shrugged her shoulders. "Sorry."

He sat back in his seat and slowly straightened his posture while returning the glare Trisha's way.

The headlights behind her car startled her. Assuming it was someone that might help, she took a nearby tissue to her face and checked her appearance in the rear-view mirror. Being cautious, she double checked that her doors were locked and cracked her window slightly on the passenger side since that was the safest way for anyone to approach her vehicle away from oncoming traffic.

"Is everything okay, Miss?"

"Yes, I'm fine. I was just looking for the roadside assistance number," she said, avoiding eye contact as the lie rolled off her tongue. "Thanks for checking on me. I'm good."

The stranger didn't move or respond. Trisha ignored his presence while uneasiness crept up on her. A nervous urge came over her, and she briefly imagined something dreadful taking place. Maybe this stranger had a weapon and preyed on women stranded on the side of the road and she would be his next victim. With her mouth set in a determined line and eyebrows furrowed, she tried to appear fearless and courageous in front of him.

"Trisha? I thought that was you girl."

Her eyebrow shot upward, and her eyes widened, but she still couldn't make out his face against the night sky. His outfit looked like he was headed to some kind of classy dinner.

The stranger knelt down and pushed his forehead toward the window. "Trisha, it's me."

Glee rocked her core, and all the air rushed out of her lungs for a brief second. Trisha held her chest and muttered, "Jason!"

"Yeah, let me in." Jason looked just as surprised and ecstatic as her. As he got in, Trisha felt the cold from the night air. He reached over and gave her a hug, sending more cold air her way.

"How have you been? I can't believe it's you."

"Great, how about you?" she asked feeling a little reluctant that she ran into Jason of all people on the side of the road, yet content that she wasn't all alone and had help from a familiar face.

"Good, but now that I'm sitting here with you, I'm floating a little bit, you know? It's been a long time." Her body became warm as she looked at his beautiful bright smile and gazed into his brown eyes. Snapping out of her trance, she turned away sweeping her shoulder-length hair away from her face. There was an awkward silence as Jason sat in the passenger seat comfortably. The space between them felt still and soothing. She tried to divert his attention to avoid having any discussions about unfinished business from the past.

Trisha looked around her car. "Umm, so I better find this number. I appreciate you stopping."

"Now hold on. I got you," Jason interjected while reaching for the passenger door handle.

Trisha responded in a soft-spoken voice, attempting to pretend she didn't want his help.

"No, Jason. You've got on a suit and this leather jacket. That's okay. I got it."

A laugh escaped his lips as he closed the passenger door. Eagerly, she reached with her left hand for the latch under the dashboard. After hearing the sound of a heavy pop, she waited for further directions. Jason signaled for her to turn on the engine. The car muffled and stopped.

"Try it one more time," he shouted. The same muffled noise repeated and stopped. Jason slammed the hood shut and got back in the car escaping the crisp air. He blew his breath into his hands for warmth.

"Are you okay?" Trisha asked.

"What are you talking about girl? Of course, I'm good."

Trisha giggled.

"What?"

"Nothing Jason. It's just good to see you."

"It's really good to see you, too." Minutes passed without either of them uttering a word. "I was going to keep going. I'm glad I stopped. I must be in a good neighborly mood today."

Trisha laughed affectionately remembering how Jason's talented persona could change anyone's sorrow to glee with his silly antics and quick responses.

"I'm serious. Any other day I would have looked over and kept driving."

"Anyway, Jason." Trisha's cheeks began to ache from smiling so big.

"See, that's what I miss. You smiling at me, just like that." Trisha noticed how Jason's facial expression shifted. The awkward silence they shared before returned. It was evident feelings still lingered between them. Her smile slowly faded, and she focused her attention straight ahead, refusing to allow that door to open.

"So, what have you been doing with yourself these days? Look at you. I'm digging the attire you've got on."

Bounce Back From Tragedy

Jason brushed his suit and groomed his mustache. "You like this old thing?" He waited patiently for her to turn toward his direction again. Jason demanded her attention, gazing deeply into her eyes seductively. "I'm a financial counselor."

"Really! Ok now, toot-toot," Trisha teased playfully as Jason looked at his hands with an embarrassed grin. "That's wonderful. I'm proud of you."

"Thanks Trish, so what about you? What are you doing now, Miss Thang? You look amazing."

He must be blind if he can't see how puffy and red my eyes are, she thought.

"Well, I used my hard-earned business degree to own and operate my own boutique. It's not much, but it pays the bills, and I love it."

"That's what's up! You always had that style and fashion sense about you. You used to help me pick out my clothes and kept me looking fly from head to toe back in high school."

Trisha burst out laughing, while shaking her head. "Aw man, I had no talent for matching whatsoever back then... so, what did your pops say? Wait let me guess."

She lowered her voice to mimic her father. "You need to be a nurse, doctor, or something. There is more to life than just shopping and buying clothes." They snickered in unison.

Jason pretended to be her father and went into coach mode. "What? You think this is funny? Okay, alright, let me tell you something. Losing games isn't funny. I don't lose. I win. If I'm not winning, then I'm not happy. And when I'm not happy, you all will run. You got that. Feet in motion, GO!"

"I'm telling you, your dad had this vein thing right here." Jason pointed to his forehead as Trisha giggled hysterically. "We used to think that thing was going to jump out and get us, for real."

"Jason we better stop. I got to get this car taken care of," Trisha said, while still laughing.

"Oh, the car. Hey, listen," he said in a playful tone while shaking his head, "Trish, the car's not moving. It's smoking under the hood and everything."

She rolled her eyes as she thought about all the things she needed to do tomorrow and the rest of the week. Having her car in the shop wasn't one of them.

She exhaled in disappointment. "Not good. I need to call a tow truck."

"Trish, what?" Jason pointed to himself. "Hey, I got this. I'll call the tow truck and get things straight for you. On me, my treat."

"Anyway, Jason!"

"On me. My treat," Jason repeated letting Trisha know that he was serious. "Let's get in my car." They walked a few feet to Jason's brand-new black Benz.

"Oh really?" Trisha said as she closed the door on the passenger side.

Bounce Back From Tragedy

"Oh yeah, this is how I do it." Jason flashed a proud smile. "Listen, I was headed this way on business, but where were you headed? Home is that way," Jason questioned, pointing his finger in the opposite direction.

"Home for me is this way." Trisha pointed forward. "See home stopped being home a long time ago. I don't make it that way much, but I did this weekend, and I know I won't be back for a real good while this time."

Jason took in as much air as possible before letting it out slowly. Trisha could see that he was distraught. She knew why and chose to say nothing more as she replayed the conversation with her father over tonight's dinner.

***

"You're punishing me, aren't you?"

"What daddy?"

"You're punishing me, right? From high school? Look, I did the best I could, and now you've got to move on with your life. We all know your independent, male-hating attitude is a show."

"Punishing you?" Trisha surveyed the dinner table before turning her attention back to her father. "You knew exactly what he did to me, and you didn't do anything about it. You covered over his wrong while portraying yourself as my pimp!" An immediate hush fell over the dinner table.

"You two stop it! Not here," her mother yelled.

"Why mom? Huh?" Trisha snapped. She turned directly toward her father. "You knew! You asked me to come along for the big game out of state. You said you could use an extra hand. You sent me into that locker room to get the rest of the equipment after checking that no one was in there, when you knew. You knew it."

"That's enough, Trisha." Her father slapped the kitchen table.

"No daddy," Trisha shouted back coming out of her seat and pointing at him. "I kept telling you how he would talk to me in school, always calling me a stuck-up heifer because I didn't have a thing for him like every other girl. He would even grab my behind from time-to-time. I had to get in his face and talk trash only to hope that he would stop. You know why he took so much delight in harassing me? Do you daddy? Because he knew you wouldn't do a thing to his star player. You knew daddy. You set up all the pieces."

"Enough," he said in a controlled, irate tone.

"And when I called and called, and screamed for you, you didn't come. You never came. And when you finally asked what happened, you took his words over mine." She shook her head as she sat back down. "Your only daughter. That's how I lost my virginity, by it being stolen."

Trisha paused and looked around at the family pictures on the wall. "It's funny how all of a sudden, we had more money after he went straight to the pros. You bought me a car." Her

Bounce Back From Tragedy

father sat there quietly knowing there was nothing he could say because it was all true. "Daddy, we never talked about it. All those expensive gifts were a cover up."

Trisha looked around at the rest of the table. "Every last one of you at this table have benefited in some way from it. Uncle Carl, daddy bought you that fishing boat." Uncle Carl turned away and began to scratch the back of his head nervously.

"So, don't any of you tell me how to run my life." Trisha stood up one final time. "That's why I don't come around much. I'm out of here."

"Trisha." Jason reached over and grabbed her hand.

"It's okay, Jason." She cut him off quickly. Jason looked at her as if trying to decide if he should continue to speak or back down.

"Trisha," he tried again. "I'm sorry I wasn't there to protect you."

"Jason, it's not your fault."

"You don't understand Trish, that dude…" Jason squeezed her hand tightly. "He always thought he could do whatever to whomever he wanted. I mean the whole team knew he was like that. The locker room talk was always just over the top. I should have done something." A tear dropped from his eye. "I never thought in a million years that you would be the one to get hurt."

"Jason, it was years ago. Let's just drop it."

"Please let me finish," he begged. "One time your name came up. I had already told him to keep your name out of his mouth, and we would repeatedly have words over you. Well on this day, before the game out of state, I just had enough. He said something foul about you. I turned around and ran toward him full speed. I was just so angry. I literally picked him up in the air off his feet and slammed him down on the locker room floor and just started hitting him as hard and as fast as I could. It took four guys to pull me off that dude."

Trisha tried to keep collected, but she couldn't hold back. Tears began to stream down her face. It seemed like a movie. However, she felt inner peace for the first time. A calmness fell over her entire body, and she let go of her pain that very moment.

"That's why I wasn't at the game that night. I would have found a way to be there if I knew you were tagging along. I never told you, but that's why your dad kicked me off the team. When I heard about what happened to you, I didn't know how to deal, and you wouldn't talk to me about it." Jason looked at Trisha in her eyes to make sure he still had her attention. "You're the reason I went to USC. I had to be there and make sure you succeeded. I needed to see you thrive, and I'm so proud of you because you stayed focus through all the pain. I put in overtime work to make you smile, and to make you laugh. You may not have realized it, but you were helping me to heal every time you did."

Bounce Back From Tragedy

Trisha felt overwhelmed with joy. She didn't know how to respond as he continued.

"I was in so much pain when I learned about what happened, and then seeing how he got nothing but glory and fame afterward, going pro. I just..." Jason turned away and took a deep breath while grinding his teeth. "I just..."

Trisha chimed in. "I get it Jason, I do. Thank you for telling me this. It helps." She reached over and kissed him tenderly on the cheek. The stillness returned between them for a brief moment.

Okay, time to lighten the mood.

"Sooo, Jason, what's the lady in your life going to say about all this quality time we've spent together? Aww, you're in trouble."

Jason smiled a little and turned toward Trisha. "There is no lady in my life Trish. You know what? I wanted it back then, but I knew the timing wasn't right. And I'm positive that I want it even more right now. I'm hoping you want that job."

Buried sensations aroused. The feeling seemed foreign. Trisha never allowed herself to have romantic feelings for anyone, but this flutter developing inside her felt better than any feeling she had experienced before.

She tossed an alluring glance his way. "I do. When do I start?"

Jason smiled as if he'd just won an Olympic gold medal. "Right now."

He leaned closer to her as she turned toward him, and they connected face-to-face for the first time.

Deception

I'm so sick of this! Joy thought to herself as she continued to rummage through Luke's briefcase. After careful examination, she only found work-related memos and documents. The item she expected to find was missing, which infuriated her even more. Joy slammed the briefcase shut while letting it fall to ground. She hastily wrapped her long jet-black hair in a bun with a hair tie from their elegant dresser and stormed out the bedroom. She headed straight for the office down the hall, stomping with each step until she reached the cozy warm-colored nook.

Joy stood in the threshold. She held her ivory arms and stared at the tan walls while her gray-colored eyes began to water. She had hoped to turn this room into a nursery, but Luke continually made it clear that the timing wasn't right for a child. She questioned herself in agony. *Why is it such a crime to want to give birth to his child?*

She glanced around the room and vigorously went for his miniature file cabinet located behind his cherry wood desk. After plopping down in his leather rolling chair and pulling out the top drawer, she began to carefully go through his files. She would pull one out, mark her spot with a pen, and turn to place the file on the desktop across from his metallic Mac computer. She looked thru each file carefully, trying to make sense of her burning intuition that Luke had multiple secrets. *Why?* He hadn't done anything like this before. He embodied the classic good guy. Now their fairy tale marriage appeared to be coming to a screeching halt.

As Joy searched through each and every file, she began to lose her patience. Her forehead, neck, and underarms began to perspire, and her dry eyes stung even more. She had already spent half the morning looking in every one of Luke's pants pockets, coat pockets, suit pockets, laundry, and drawers. *Seven years of marriage, seven years of marriage,* she kept thinking to herself repeatedly.

After searching through the bottom file cabinet and coming up short, Joy let out an extended scream that echoed throughout the four corners of their sophisticated suburban home. A sudden epiphany hit her. Joy jumped up with a renewed energy and hurried down the carpeted stairs through the granite kitchen and into the garage while grabbing the car key hanging from the petite wooden rack.

Luke had taken their Toyota Sedan on his four day business trip and left behind his Cadillac. He had gone on business trips faithfully every three weeks for the past four months. Long enough for Joy to notice and feel the pattern of deceit. She searched through every inch of the car, but it was clean and clear of anything suspicious.

Joy began to pace back and forth in the garage, her mind replaying Luke's excuses over the past few months. As she looked into his warm blue eyes and admired his light brown skin, he'd tell her, "Sorry babe, I need to go out of town again this weekend for another business meeting. I'm working a big project." Or, "Awe babe, *I'm sorry*. I didn't expect to head out so soon."

Joy pulled down boxes out of desperation and searched all the shelves in the garage while her chest tightened as a panic attack began to ensue. Within minutes Joy began to feel a horrific rumble in her stomach. It was well past lunch time, and she hadn't eaten breakfast. The bags under her eyes were heavy from last night's tossing and turning. All she could focus on was the sensation of betrayal that engulfed her heart. Joy had enough! She was tired of Luke being out of town. And when he was away, he rarely answered her phone calls except to tell her he was on his way back home.

Exhausted and breathing heavily, Joy walked sluggishly into the kitchen toward the refrigerator. She opened the door and embraced the cool breeze coming from within. She reached for a salad and bottled water, slid out the stool with her foot, and sat at the island that graced the middle of the kitchen. She planned her next move as she partook of her salad.

Without cleaning her spot, Joy stumbled back toward the garage door. She grabbed her purse on the way and climbed into her Subaru Legacy, pausing briefly to ask herself, *Do I really want to do this?* Joy backed out of the driveway and headed for the main road that led to the interstate and gave her a straight shot from Springfield, Illinois to the heart of downtown Chicago.

Three hours later, Joy exited off I-55 and traveled toward the five-star Katterburg Hotel where Luke mentioned he was staying. As she spotted the hotel signage in the distance that rested on top of the eighteenth floor, her heart began to beat faster and faster. She was moving off pure emotion, without any forethought. Her mind wandered as she thought about the other woman. *What does she look like? Is she prettier? What does she do that I don't do? Did I bring this upon myself? I thought I was a good wife.*

Joy wiped the continuous stream that flowed down her cheeks as she pulled into the half circle roundabout of the hotel. An adolescent dressed in a white collared shirt and black pants appeared and opened the door for her. He seemed startled by her worn out, sweaty appearance, but he remained silent as she rose from the car and placed her keys in his hand without speaking a word. Joy patted her hair in an effort to look a little less frightful. She took a long deep breath before walking into the magnificent, shiny, chic lobby adorned with chandeliers, beautiful flooring, and a restaurant.

Bounce Back From Tragedy

As Joy approached the receptionist desk, she was greeted with raised eyebrows and confused looks. Clearly, they thought that she was either lost or some kind of addict.

"How can we help you?" a clean shaved, well-dressed gentleman asked from behind the counter with disdain and a deep tremble in his voice.

Joy attempted to convey a normal disposition before she replied. "Oh my, what a day! I'm Joy Martin, Luke Martin's wife. I misplaced my hotel key. I just need to get up there and get some rest."

The front desk personnel's disposition softened immediately when he heard the name Luke Martin. "Oh! Of course, ma'am!" he said, clapping his hands together in excitement. "One moment. Here is a key for room 1822. How is Mr. Martin feeling?" He reached over and began rubbing Joy's hand. Joy glanced at the other two workers and noticed their initial facial expressions of disgust were replaced with sincere smiles.

Joy responded with an awkward fake grin. "He's hanging in there." At the sound of those words, the female receptionist, whose hair was swept up in a neat pony tail, sighed while placing her hand on her chest.

"Well, you just be sure to let us know if you need anything. Anything at all."

"Thank you. I sure will," Joy responded while reaching for the hotel key. *Weird.* She turned away and rolled her eyes as she headed for the middle hallway that gave her access to the double row of brass elevators. Overcome by emotions, she almost broke down in tears again but managed to hold it in.

A soft ding behind her sounded. Joy turned and entered, taking closer steps toward the truth. The ride to the eighteenth floor was slow and lonely. When she reached her destination, the elevator doors opened, and she was standing face-to-face with a very attractive women wearing a short, tight, red dress that showed her perfect figure, the model type. Joy glared with rage as the unsuspecting woman glanced at her momentarily and pardoned herself to step around Joy and into the elevator. Joy then stepped out and turned around to face the prestigious women. While the doors closed, she glared just long enough to be greeted with an eye roll.

What if that's her? That could be her!

Joy's legs became heavy. Reaching for the decorative table nearby, she regained balance. She headed down the hallway after gathering what dignity she could muster up. Her heart pounded and a knot formed in her throat. Her chest began to burn as the room numbers increased...1812...1816...1820...1822. She took a deep breath and exhaled slowly while trying to listen for a brief moment; however, she couldn't hear any sound through the thickness of the heavy wooden door. She took another deep breath, holding it a little longer before releasing slowly.

Bounce Back From Tragedy

She raised her trembling right hand, which kept a firm grasp on the room key. Her forehead began to drip sweat. Then, she slid the plastic key into the slit above the door handle, watched for the light to turn green, and barged in only to be greeted by a dark, tranquil room, without any occupants. The evening light from the sun allowed Joy to find the nearby light switch with ease. She flipped the switch and reached for her head with one hand. In a rage, she grabbed her Louis Vuitton purse, which rested in the crease of her elbow, flung it toward the wall, and dropped down while more tears streamed down her face.

Joy stood up and surveyed the room. It was evident that the maid handled the room with care as the beds looked nice and neatly tucked. The table and dresser tops sparkled, and there was a soft scent of lilac in the air. A note next to the 32-inch flat screen television read: *Please enjoy your stay, let me know if you need anything, Rita.*

Joy looked at the bed. The idea of falling asleep pleased her. She fantasized about waking up to Luke holding her, apologizing for all the time he spent away and his suspicious behavior. She would explain that she only came all this way to surprise him and get some attention, which was somewhat true.

She refocused on what brought her here and began rustling through the drawers. There were no ties or dress socks— only a pair of jeans, sweat pants, basketball shorts, and a few plain shirts. She backed up and looked at the clothes hanging up by the door entryway. Nothing. Not even one suit. Confirmed! This was definitely not a business trip. Joy eagerly tried to figure out more pieces to the puzzle. Luke had always been a well-dressed man. Joy sat on the bed confused. *Something's not right. He would have packed nicer attire if he was seeing another woman. No suits, but why didn't he pack any name brand clothing?*

She saw two different brands of suitcases on the floor. She knew the black, professional suitcase belonged to Luke, but she didn't recognize the other plaid, worn, outdated bag. She walked over to the awkward duffle bag lying on the floor, kneeled down and unzipped it slowly. She cautiously reached inside and noticed everything was balled up without care. Nothing fancy, just casual attire, a few khaki pants and collard shirts. She stopped and placed her hands on her hip. *Who does this belong to? Who is he here with and what are they doing?* Joy opened a small pocket. It was stuffed with men's jewelry. Jewelry she recognized. *Zack! But...Zack?*

Joy stood up. She franticly fished for her purse, which was halfway under the bed positioned closest to the wall on the other side of the room. She placed it on the bed, plopped down next to it, and reached for her silver Apple smartphone. She held down the number four to dial her sister-in-law Bonnie. Instead of hearing the southern twang of Bonnie's sweet, delicate voice, her call immediately went to an automated voicemail message. She hung up and closed her eyes until she felt a vibration.

Working. What's up?

Nothing. I just need to get ahold of Zack.

Bounce Back From Tragedy

???? You know he's on a business trip with Luke???

What in the world is going on? What are they up to? She glanced at Luke's suitcase, got up, and dragged it to where she was sitting on the bed.

It felt light and flimsy. She placed it beside her. Still confused and bewildered, Joy unzipped it hurriedly and looked inside only to find a few more socks and a couple pairs of briefs. Her chest deflated while rubbing her thighs with both hands, trying calm her racing heartbeat. Joy replayed the discussion she had with Luke just days before.

"Again Luke! Really! Are you kidding me?"

"I know babe. It's just another business meeting. I'll only be gone a few days. I promise to make it up to you when I get back." Luke's smooth lips kissed hers while his warm hands rubbed her cheeks. *"I promise."*

Joy began to inspect the suitcase more closely sliding her hand in the zipper inside. She felt something and heard a crumble. Her body became fearful and froze. Slowly she pulled out the folded colorful contents, opened the wad of papers, and found herself looking at pamphlets of what appeared to be medical paperwork. She read the title of the first brochure. "You're a survivor!" Her heart galloped faster than it had the entire day. *What if... Could he have...*She looked at the title of the next pamphlet: "Facts and Resources—All You Need to Know About Non-Hodgkin Lymphoma"

"What! What is this? What's going on?" Her voice squealed, loud and dry in the empty room. She opened the pamphlet and skimmed over the symptoms, diagnosis, and treatment options. Her chest became tight and she began to find it hard to breathe once more.

Joy wasn't sure if she felt relief or frustration. Luke wasn't having an affair. He was sick! But why would he hide something so serious? So important? Joy's body became flushed with jealousy, sorrow, and anger. She laid back on the bed. This is not what she expected to find. She wished that she would have discovered that Luke was having an affair instead. *Is he going to die? Is my husband dying? Why didn't I notice?* Luke looked the same after each trip. He would constantly come home refreshed and in good spirits. Joy's suspicions grew after each return.

Joy's bottom lip quivered, and she covered her face with her shaking hands. Time passed. She dragged herself off the bed and walked over to the open window. The sunset made the green landscape of the park glow beautifully. A slight grin rose up on one side of her face as she watched two small children playing below with their mother sitting nearby, next to a stroller, on a cemented bench. Joy touched her mid-section and lowered her head. *Why is this happening?* She folded her arms, tilted her head back, and closed her eyes. When she opened them, a bright light nearby the park caught her attention, but it was partially blocked by a building in front of it. However, the bright red cross on a lit white background told her all she needed to know. A hospital. Joy turned from the window and opened the small door connected to the dresser. She found a mini refrigerator full of water bottles and snacks. She grabbed a bottle and checked herself out in the mirror. Joy was almost unrecognizable. She went into the bathroom to freshen up and wet her hair. After grabbing her purse, she glanced in the mirror one last time. *Better!*

Outside the hotel, Joy noticed that the small children and their mother had left. The fresh air and breeze from the late evening surrounded Joy and felt inviting. She headed toward the bright sign at a steady pace. Her sneakers, jeans, and basic top didn't paint the real depiction of Joy's true fashion sense.

Soon Joy stood in front of the Chicago University Hospital. The campus was vast and medical buildings were stationed at her left and right. Joy walked into what appeared to be the main hospital entrance. Medical professionals and patrons bustled around the busy setting. Some carried on in conversations with laughter while others walked in silence with worry plastered across their faces.

Several women were dressed in teal suit jackets and white blouses at the big round information station. She walked a few feet toward the desk, and before she could ask for assistance, they greeted her with a friendly smile.

"Hello Miss, can I help you locate something or someone?" The aged woman had a pleasant disposition and studied Joy through the glasses resting on her face, while waiting for a response.

Uneasy and emotionally Joy responded. "Yes. I'm looking for Luke. Luke Martin."

"Luke Martin." Joy watched as the woman's fingers punched the keyboard and her eyes searched her computer screen. "Okay Miss. He is in outpatient oncology."

Joy almost started to cry when she heard the word oncology.

"Okay, and where is that?"

Her hand pointed to the side. "You want to go through these doors here. Make a right, and then take that long hallway all the way to the end. There will be an automatic double set of doors on your left that will read outpatient oncology."

"Yes, thank you!" As Joy took the long hallway, she couldn't help but notice patients being pushed in wheelchairs; some were missing hair. Others were attached to fluids on stretchers, and some walked with assistance from staff or family. When Joy reached the automatic double doors, she stalled. As her hand raised to hit the metal plate, the doors swung open in her direction.

"Oh, I'm sorry dear," a gray-haired older woman said as she passed by Joy.

"No problem." She walked slowly inside.

Joy glanced around and noticed that she was in a waiting room area. One side was a secretary chamber along with a single metal door next to it. Connecting chairs aligned the room in small clusters. As Joy approached the secretary station, she caught a familiar glimpse. She turned her head to see Zack staring at her with his eyes widened in shock while holding a soda in his hand. His face expression suddenly changed as his eyes and brows lowered out of guilt.

Joy stood there enraged while examining his face and disposition. He walked toward her. "Joy," he said in a sympathetic tone.

She pointed her finger at him, suppressing the urge to slap him. "Don't! Don't you dear!"

"But Joy, how did you-"

She cut him off in a low tone, trying hard not to make a scene in the middle of the waiting room. "How dare you? You helped him hide this from me."

"Listen Joy, you're my little sister and I love you. But I love him like a brother too. We roomed together in college. You would have never met him if it wasn't for me. The treatments are just one day, with another day or two to recover. I'm trying to help you both." Zack pleaded.

"Shut! Up! Don't you dare try to justify this." Joy's anger seemed to terrify Zack. She pointed her index finger straight at him and motioned abrasively. "Take me to my husband, now."

Zack held up both hands, motioning a surrender. "Sure Joy." He took her through the metal door that led to the treatment area. "He's behind that curtain over there. The one that reads three. Only one visitor can be in here at a time, so I better step out."

"Zack," Joy whispered.

"Yes Joy."

"I can't believe you did this to me," she expressed looking into her sibling's matching gray eyes.

He shook his head. "I'm sorry. I didn't know what to do." Joy began to walk away.

"Hey Joy." She stopped and looked back. "He was just trying to protect you. That's all." Joy looked at him without any response and then turned back around and headed toward the curtain. She was scared of what she would find behind it.

She stepped in to find Luke hunched over to one side of a tan hospital recliner chair with an IV going into his left forearm. Joy was overcome with sadness. His eyes flickered a little and then he squinted. Weak from the treatment, he called out to her. "Babe, babe is that you." She walked to his side and began stroking his sandy-tamed hair.

"Shhhh. Yes baby, I'm here."

"Babe…" Luke struggled to speak. "What are you doing here?"

"Shhh, not now."

"I just didn't want you to worry. We just lost your father last year and then the miscarriage a few years ago. I refuse to see you depressed like you were before. I thought I was going to lose you this last time." Joy covered his mouth with her finger tenderly, and he kissed it lovingly.

"We'll talk later." She set her purse down next to the treatment chair and climbed in next to him where there was just enough room for a tight squeeze. He slowly wrapped his arm around her and laid his head on her chest. He held onto Joy like a sick child clings onto his mother.

"Joy," he said still struggling to form words. "I love you so much!"

"I love you too, Luke. We'll get through this from now on together.

Memoir of a Slut

I'm lying in our bed, looking at the city's skyline from on top of the hill where our home resides. I've always loved how the glass sliding doors lead to the balcony. I normally step outside and inhale the fresh air of a new day before I do anything else, but not today. Today I'm tucked in my silk sheets that sometimes make me feel like I'm a princess floating on air, as my back and arm throb. I can't help but question where my place is in this world. Who am I?

"Instead of lying there feeling sorry for yourself, why don't you get up and clean this place up, Lauryn?" The sharp tone belongs to my arrogant, cowardly husband, Mr. Braxton L. Adams IV, owner of Adams brokerage firm.

A few moments later I hear the front double doors to our oversized San Franciscan home close and the engine starts on Mr. Adam's third sports car, a bright yellow Ferrari. I arise slowly and proceed across our wooden bedroom floor toward our master bathroom. I hate wooden floors. Sometimes the floor feels so cold and hard, just like our marriage.

Bounce Back From Tragedy

***

When I first met Braxton, the only thing that bothered me was his name. I took a summer internship my junior year working for my father's corporation Morgan Properties to earn some extra cash. Daddy owned a variety of apartment buildings, subdivisions, and commercial real estate. He always wanted me to go to school and pursue law, but all I wanted to do was live a simple life and teach elementary students, so I pursued a degree in education instead.

I enjoyed the best internship imaginable in college because I could come and go when I wanted. I worked hard, but I played hard too. I just didn't find anything wrong with going shopping during lunchtime every once in a while.

Half-way through my internship, my father's 2:00 appointment walked in on one hot July afternoon. Braxton. His walk immediately caught my attention. It was solid and powerful, confident, and welcoming as he approached my desk located on the side of the elevator. Braxton wore a black, top of the line Gucci double breasted suit with a white collared shirt and paisley tie. He was just over six feet with very distinct features. It was obvious that Native American was heavy in his lineage, although his skin had a rich dark brown tone. He looked so focused and determined that day but handsome in every way possible.

"Hello. How can I help you?" I asked, although I already knew he was my father's next appointment.

"Hi, I'm here to see Mr. Morgan. We have a 2:00," he replied. His wide smile revealed his perfect teeth.

"Ok, you can have a seat. He'll be with you shortly."

I called my father's office and notified him of his next appointment. My father took Braxton to his office, and one hour later, he showed him out toward the elevator. I heard something vague from about 15 feet away as the elevator door closed. It seemed like my dad and Braxton were going to pick up their conversation over dinner. My father seemed eager as he walked over to my desk.

"Baby girl, why don't you go on home and freshen up? I need you to put on something nice. Very nice. I'm going to take you along to dinner tonight with the fella that just left out of here."

"Daddy, I have plans tonight. My roommate from college is coming to visit me for the weekend. I told you that before," I whined.

"That's right, that's right. Listen, I need to borrow you for a few hours and then you can go hang out with your friend. I'll tell your mother to give her the keys to the guest house and you can catch up with her later."

"Borrow me? Daddy what does that mean?" It was clear that my father had arranged something without me knowing it. Let's just say, a distraction. I'm sure he didn't expect it and neither did I, but Braxton and I felt a strong connection that night and the connection grew. I found myself falling in love for the first time shortly after our encounter.

***

As I glare at myself in the mirror, I don't even recognize the woman staring back at me. She is depressed, lonely, and in so much pain on the inside and out. I decide to shower and get going with my day. Braxton knows that I keep the house clean. He just wants to find something to complain about, so I decide I'll rearrange some pictures and furniture instead hoping to appease him. Before I can get in the shower, the phone rings.

"I can't believe you. What have you done?"

"Hello mother," I answer in an irritated tone. I'm not surprised by the call.

"After all that man has done for you, you treat him like you do. When will you learn to keep your mouth shut?"

"Good-bye mother."

I hang up the phone. I can't handle her. At least not right now. I close my eyes and think about the first time it all started. I met his other side.

***

We were still newlyweds, and Braxton took me out to eat at our favorite hole in the wall spot, Maxine's Jumping Savoy. After dinner and drinks, we danced all night, laughing and swaying in each other's embrace. Before we left, Braxton ran into his old friend Lester. Braxton and Lester said their hellos and gave each other brotherly hugs, and then Braxton introduced me. Lester gave me a friendly hug, and then they resumed with catching up.

On the car ride home, I began to feel uneasy. I couldn't understand why the mood had changed. Braxton was distant and upset as he drove his Mercedes aggressively.

"You like embarrassing me, don't you?" Braxton sternly questioned.

"Embarrassing you?" I questioned. "I don't know what you mean. Sweetheart, what did I do?"

"So, you're a liar too. Your father never told me that. That man knew how much I wanted you." He looked over at me with red and dilated eyes. "What man wouldn't? You're drop dead gorgeous. Beautiful and brown, packing in the front and the back, long luscious legs. You can't help but flirt, can you?"

The tension grew tighter, and I couldn't process what was happening. The more I tried to explain that I wasn't flirting, the more upset Braxton became. The strange behavior was bewildering and made it hard for me to exhale. Although we lived twenty-five minutes away from Maxine's, we seemed to reach home within fifteen.

"Hurry up and get your behind in the house. We're going to fix this right now!" He ordered, pulling me by the arm.

I began to get worried. Very worried. We walked through our heavy double pine doors. He slammed it shut and hit me with a closed fist in my abdomen. I immediately fell to my knees, and my hands slapped against the glazed marble that covered our entire first floor. I felt like the earth stopped spinning on its axis. Everything seemed still. I couldn't breathe, and I held my stomach while aching in pain trying to make sense of what was taking place.

"You like throwing yourself at men. You like to embarrass me. You don't think I have any feelings," Braxton hollered as he stood over me like a hungry wolf, ready to attack.

"I wasn't flirting with anyone. I'm sorry if..."

Before I could get another word out of my mouth, he snatched my shoulder-length bob into a knot and struck me several times in my face with his opposite hand. I thought he was trying to kill me. That moment felt like a scene that only happened in movies— not to me. Each blow caused more pain than the one prior. It felt like an eternity had passed before the striking stopped, and Braxton strutted away. I fell down limp and exhausted on the marble floor once again. I rested at our entryway until the room stopped spinning. I couldn't do anything but cry, so I wailed quietly while running my hands over my sore and bloody face.

Our two years of dating had felt like a fairy tale. Braxton and I took our time before joining together in matrimony. But I learned that night I didn't really know him. Eventually, I mustered up the strength to get on my knees. Still in pain, I crawled down the hall and reached up to the key rack only to find it empty. I sat and began to cry again. I didn't know what to do. I crawled back toward the door and found my handheld Coach purse that he threw against the wall earlier. Scrambling for my phone, I placed a call.

I waited by the door until I heard the car pull up, the latest Bentley on the market. It was now near dawn. I stumbled out the door and down the three cemented stairs that graced our main entrance. I didn't even allow mother to park before I was at her passenger door trying to gain entry to the slow moving vehicle. She looked at me liked a frozen statue with concern plastered all over her face. She stopped and jumped out the car.

"No momma, get back in the car, unlock the door. I just need to go," I pleaded. She walked around the hood of the car and got a closer look at my face.

"What happened to you?" she screamed. "What did he do to you?"

"Momma, I just need to go. Get me out of here."

My mother ignored my petition and began to walk up the steps toward the front door, but Braxton appeared before she could enter the house.

"Hey mom." He reached over to give her a kiss on the cheek as usual. "It's not what it looks like. We just had a little disagreement, that's all."

"It's not what it looks like. Have you seen her face?" my mother hollered. "We are honoring the memory of her father tonight. You're the spokesmen! How can she go anywhere looking like that?"

"I'll just tell them she's sick or something," he replied nonchalantly.

I couldn't believe that my mother didn't rip into him. I couldn't believe that she didn't get me out of there. As they continued to talk, I stumbled around the hood to the driver's side to sit down and rest. I heard my mother's commanding voice.

"Lauryn don't get in my car. You're bleeding honey, and I just had my car detailed. Hold on a minute."

I was in utter disbelief and despair. I tried to walk down the hilly driveway and stumbled into the grass.

"Look at her! Look at her! You can't have my child if you're going to treat her like this." Braxton's reply was disturbing and revealing at the same time.

"Don't tell me what I can't have when I pay your mortgage. You're nothing but a gold digger who married for money and got with an ambitious man who didn't know how to invest wisely. I own her, and really, I own you too. As a matter of fact, you tell your daughter to stop acting like a slut, hugging all on men we meet in bars, and we won't have problems like this."

My mother's whole disposition changed. At that moment I missed my father immensely. I missed him like I never missed him before.

"What about tonight?" she asked in a softer tone.

"Call one of those make-up artists to come. She doesn't look that bad," he replied with lack of remorse. I heard my mother's footsteps approaching.

"Lauryn, pull yourself together and get inside and please this man," she said in a shaky voice. "If you're going to act like a slut, you'll be treated like one." The quiver in her throat was clear, and although we never got along because she despised the nurturing relationship between my father and I, she didn't love me enough to protect me. She never did. "I'll see you tonight. Arrive beautiful." She got back into her Bentley and drove off. Braxton came over to me and knelt down. His rough hands examined my face.

"I'm sorry. I just lost my cool, but don't worry. I'll never do this again." He picked me up securely, held me close to his chest, and carried me inside.

***

I decide to soak in the jacuzzi instead of taking a shower. I need to relax. As I sit in this pool of warm water covered with floating bubbles, I begin to think about the times in my life when I was the happiest. All of my honor roll assemblies, dance recitals, and plays. My father made each one. If my mother showed up, she was either coming late or leaving early. I remembered how my dad and I would take our special drive north after each of my honor roll assemblies. It was our special place. The town was located between two forest preserves. We would have a picnic on a hill top that overlooked a small independent bank, play patty cake, go hiking, and finish up the weekend with our secret number song followed by our secret hand shake. The song was my favorite when I was younger. My father would start off the song happily and carefree.

"Me and You."

Then I'd chimed in. "You and Me."

Then together we'd sing the rest. "Together, forever, no matter, whatever. 57-89-76-2-2-3-3, something just for you from me."

I haven't sung that song in years. Not since my early adolescence, although daddy would continue to hum it around me and tickle me afterward. He never let me forget. Together, forever, no matter, whatever. 57-89-76-2-2-3-3, something just for you from me.

I begin to hum the song to myself over and over. Suddenly, I rise up so quickly that a little water falls onto the floor. I sing the song again quietly and slowly to myself.

"Me and You. You and Me. Together, forever, no matter, whatever."

I say the numbers even slower. "57…89…76…2-2-3-3, something just for you from me." The song is a clue. It's a bank account. There must be money in the bank near the hill.

I got it! It hits me when I least expect and when I need it the most. My father always looked out for me. His only mistake was giving approval to Braxton for my hand in marriage. This song and our long drives to our secret location was more than just daddy-daughter time.

I jump out of the jacuzzi, get dressed as fast as I can, and I grab the emergency bag that I learned to put together from one of my favorite talk shows. I get in my freshly washed silver Jaguar and head out. I drive with my adrenaline level past infinity. I drive to a new beginning

Make It Happen

I love this show. I think it's because I know I'm going to be a dancer deep down inside. I'm going to glide, twirl, arabesque across the stage, and be appreciated for my unique ability. I wish it was me now. I practice in my room every day, and I make sure to pass by Miss Lena's Dance Studio on the walk home from school to watch her ballet and jazz class through the front window. I wish I was one of the contestants on the show, standing in line, waiting on my turn to prove I've got what it takes. If I lived in New York or Chicago, I'd have my own dance crew, and everybody would know who we are. But instead, I'm in Huber Heights, Ohio, which is a long way from where I need to be.

I wish I could study all kinds of dance: ballet, jazz, hip hop, contemporary, even break dancing. For now, I love lying here across the floor and dreaming, although I'm crammed in this small two-bedroom apartment, surrounded by dirty carpet that needs cleaning and windows with bars to keep trouble out. It's just fine because I've got a vivid picture in my mind.

"Move ugly!" My aunt kicks my legs to walk by. I quickly sit up and move out of the way, pulling my knees to my chest. She sits in her old favorite reclining chair. I just try to stay calm and keep my eyes glued to the television, but I can tell it's coming. I can tell what kind of mood she's in. The black horseman enters the room. Happiness and life disappear and is replaced with anger, death, and disease. Her pupils remain fixated on me.

"You're stupid, you know that? Always watching this show. You ain't ever gonna be able to do what they can do. You just too dumb."

I pretend not to hear her. "Give me the remote," she commands with her right hand, gesturing for me to hurry up and give it to her. I place the remote softly in her hand and start to walk toward my bedroom.

"Stop there!"

I obey.

"You think you're cute, don't you? You think you're smart. Well let me tell you something… you ain't going to ever be nothing. You got that!"

I don't respond.

"Turn around and look at me. Show some respect."

I turn around. My aunt with deep red-rimmed eyes stands up wobbly and drags herself toward me, getting as close to my face as she can without touching me.

Bounce Back From Tragedy

"You used to be cute. I took you in when my sister died. I bought you all those clothes. I would do your hair nice and pretty. Feed you. And what thanks do I get? You repay me by sleeping with my man."

I turn to walk away, but my aunt grabs my arm as tightly as she can to make me stay in place. "I'm not done. You're a little whore, you know that?"

Tears start to form, which is exactly what she wants because she gives me a grim smile before continuing. "That's right. You're a little whore."

My past experience taught me that the best thing to do is stand there and take it until she is finished. But today, I don't have the silence in me. With tears running down my face, and a quiver in my voice, I defend myself by stating the facts.

"He hurt me. I didn't do anything wrong."

She releases my arm, takes a step back, and laughs. "Says you, right? I mean, that's what you say, right? I took the side of family and look where it's gotten us. We barely have anything. See, with him we had money. We weren't rich, no, but we had plenty. He took real good care of us. It's hard enough trying to make it for myself, and I've got your ugly mouth to feed too."

"I'm working!" I say. Most sixteen-year-olds spend the majority of their free time hanging out with friends or some after school activity. But I work as hard as I can at the deli, and then I give every paycheck to her.

"So, this little change you giving me don't do nothing. Maybe you should have just kept your mouth shut. You know, took one for the family. Heck, you sure 'nuff look all women, walking around with all this up here and all that back there. It wasn't like he was kin to you." She puts her finger in my face and repeats herself. "You should have kept your mouth shut."

"My momma loved me! My daddy loved me! That's why they named me Jewel because I'm somebody. I'm important. You're just evil."

"Newsflash sweetheart. Your momma died giving birth to yet another one of your sisters, and your daddy didn't want you. That's why you ended up with me. But he kept them others, didn't he? You ever think about that?"

I always think about it truthfully. I just figured he didn't keep me because I was so much older than them and I looked just like her. I'm built like her too, with the same brown eyes and smile. Maybe it brought him too much pain. I love my daddy, and my daddy loves me. Why didn't he keep me? Why did he give me to her? This witch.

"Look here," she says nonchalantly. "It's 'cause you ain't his. Stupid!"

My heart misses a beat, and my stomach whirls around like a washing machine on the spin cycle. What did she say? That just can't be true.

"You lie," I say, fighting to speak through the pain. Aunt Tina just laughs hysterically, nearly falling over.

45

Bounce Back From Tragedy

"Girl, I wish I was for your and my sake." She places a finger against her temple to reason with me. "Think about it. When was the last time he called you? Has he ever sent for you? Those little presents that used to come your way haven't come in a long time. When was the last time you saw him? At that bus station when I picked you up and he hugged you real tight? He told you things would be just fine."

I feel like I want to die.

I guess deep inside I know it's the truth.

***

I look at myself in the mirror, staring at what I've become. It's only been a few years since I turned old enough to drink. I place my hands on my face, tracing my cheeks softly, asking myself the same question I do every morning.

Who am I?

I've spent another night in New York using skills meant for excellence to have strangers pay me for fantasies and body moves set on a dim stage. Most early mornings after I touch down in this beautiful condo I bought with my well-earned money, I cry. It allows me to let out all the emptiness until I feel humanized again.

This afternoon is pretty much routine. I head out by foot and walk the eight blocks to the city library where I spend most of the remaining daylight when I have the night off. The giant pillars outside the main entrance always make me feel important when I walk past them. This library is full of so much history. It's four floors high, and there is a section for just about everything you can think of.

"Oh Jewel, honey here you go." Miss Copeland, the librarian, hands me a heavy, hard black book that requires both of my hands to carry it. "Sorry it took so long on this one babe."

"No worries." I shake the book from side to side. "I'm excited. Can't wait to get into this one. I returned the DVDs already. Thanks for having them sent for me."

I take the elevator all the way to the top floor and find my special place where I nestle all by myself at a desk near the big window. I open the old, worn out book titled, *Popular dance techniques from the 50s, 60s and 70s.* Peace surrounds me as I study how dancers used to dress and pose. This book tells me about a few dancers I can't identify. I know all there is to know about The Nicholas Brothers, Savion Glover, Debbie Allen, Paula Kelly, and Sammy Davis Jr. Now I'm learning about Anthony Dowell, Natalia Makarova, and many more.

Hours pass before I can go to my secret place and be the real me. As I head for the main library's threshold, Miss Copeland stops me again.

"I'm just waiting for my invite."

I stop. "What do you mean?"

"Well, I just figured after five years of watching you come in here just about every week, ordering books, DVDs, resource material, and let's not forget providing nice conversation from time to time, that I'd be on your invite list, that's all."

I look around still puzzled. Although we've talked here and there, Miss Copeland knows very little about who I am, and definitely nothing about what I do.

"You're not getting the hint, honey."

I bite my lip and squint my eyes as I stand there in a state of contemplation.

"I guess, I just figured that a professional dancer like yourself would have extra tickets from time to time. I'd love to see you perform."

My eyes get bigger, and a puff of air escapes my lungs out of fear. Miss Copeland has developed the wrong idea about me, and boy is she way off.

"Oh Miss Copeland, I'm not a dancer," I say, though technically I am. "I've just always admired the art form. That's all." My voice goes up an octave.

"What do you mean, you're not a dancer? If you're not, then you clearly need to be and want to be one. I've never seen anyone research one topic with as much heart and diligence as you have over the years."

Heat begins to rush to my face. I look at the floor bashfully.

"Dear, what's the problem?"

With my hands shaking and my eyes looking around in every direction, I stumble. I look at Miss Copeland and give her a straight honest answer. "A chance. I've never been given the chance. Miss Copeland whoever you think I am, I'm not that. I haven't even finished high school. I moved here with big dreams, and I guess I realized very quickly that some dreams always stay that way... a dream."

Miss Copeland's eyes become glossy and her nostrils flare. She removes her glasses and corrects her posture. "Baby make it happen. No one is going to give you anything. We don't live in that kind of world. If you are waiting for someone to hand you something, the opportunity will never come. Now you've got your health, the desire, and the know-how to do it. Stop standing still in self-pity and go make it happen."

Miss Copeland suddenly comes out of her chair and leans over the counter. She pauses for a moment, and I watch as her chest rises and falls. "Didn't finish high school, whatever! You can go back, and you can finish. In the meanwhile, stop wasting time. There will not always be an open door in life. Your job is to find the door you want and kick it open with full force!"

She sits back down slowly, puts her glasses back on, and waves her hand at me to continue on my way. "You better get started. I'll see you later."

My head swirls in confusion. It's like Miss Copeland genuinely cares. It's hard for me to identify how my body is reacting to her words of wisdom. I want to run and hug her, but my feet are telling me to move. I start walking by Miss Copeland. When I get to the doorway, I look back. Miss Copeland stares at me over the top of her glasses with her lips pressed tightly together. It startles me, so I turn and quickly exit the library.

Emotions continue to assault me when I make it outside. I sit on the vast library cemented steps while my inner being jumps with glee. Miss Copeland cares so much that she got mad and even passionate about my welfare. Why? I've known Miss Copeland for years coming and going, and yes, we would often carry on in small talk, but nothing more.

I begin to sense a presence behind me. I turn around cautiously and then jump back. Miss Copeland is standing in the doorway with her hands on her hips. I immediately get up and start jogging. I am going in the same direction I always do at this time, on most days. My feet are carrying me faster than normal. My head is no longer confused, and life seems simpler and clearer. I'm ready to tackle new experiences and act on my talent that has been locked away for so long.

Finally, I reach the building decorated with words, names, and bright colors. I climb the fence. My hands shake as I unlock the chained latch. This is my special place, and it doesn't matter that I don't have permission to be here. No one has cared about this place for decades.

I slide the door open and allow the air of the former factory to surround me. I place my things down on the floor and move to the center where the light shines through the glass ceiling. I discovered this forgotten location two years ago, and it has been my treasure ever since.

I plug my iPhone into the speakers. My neck moves from side to side and my shoulders follow along. The deep bass penetrates my soul, and I'm officially in my zone.

My body moves in ways that please me, completely different from what I do most nights. I'm driven and focused on the precise movements of my feet, legs, arms, head, and torso. I practice all my self-taught techniques starting with hip hop, jumping to ballet, stepping into tap, and finishing freely with contemporary. Today something is awakened in me.

I stop and think with sweat running down my face and chest. I decide right in this moment that I will not go back to working my nights of disgrace. That part of my life is over.

When I get home, I research all of the dance companies and dance instruction schools. Within two weeks, I find myself teaching middle school girls ballet for an after-school program. Mickie, the head instructor and owner, was very impressed with my audition and couldn't believe I had no formal training. She helped me brush up on my technique in between classes, and soon I found myself auditioning for everything dance related. A few months went by without a gig. Then I learned about a space opening up in the much-respected Maxwell Brinker's Contemporary Dance Company, and I auditioned. The next day I received the call I often dreamed about. I am officially a professional dancer.

At Brinker's, we're like family. We do more than just dance together and tour. We laugh, play, and of course, work harder than I ever have in my life. This dance company has a prestigious reputation to uphold, and I'm one of the elite.

The seasons pass, and another new year is approaching. I'm thankful for the woman I've become. I take steps through the familiar doorway I haven't seen for over a year and search for her. I look eagerly and get more impatient with each passing minute. I have them—two front row tickets.

I spot a new face working at the circulation desk. "Is Miss Copeland working today?"

"No," the librarian answers with her head hung low. "Miss Copeland is no longer with us."

Realizing the horror of her words, my pulse speeds up and I become momentarily paralyzed. The librarian notices my plight and explains. "Oh no, she retired six weeks ago and moved to California."

"Oh, okay. Well, that's great." I hunch over to take in more oxygen. I remember she always wanted to go there from some of our past conversations. She talked about her deceased husband's nice retirement plan that she would finally gain access to, and when she did, she was headed for palm trees and better weather. I'm happy for her but hate that I won't get the opportunity to thank her and tell her how much she changed my life.

I start to head out. Rehearsal time is approaching.

"Wait, what's your name?"

I turn around with a slight smile. "Jewel."

She raises her eyebrows. "Jewel!? You're Jewel? Well, these are for you."

She reaches down under her desk and hands me a package. "She told all of us that when Jewel comes by, make sure she gets this package."

I smile and thank her before I head to my car. When I open the package, I see a stack of books. The top one reads, *Preparing for the GED.* Inside the first cover is a note from Miss Copeland with very specific instructions. It lists her address, phone number, and email along with the words *don't forget to send me my ticket!*

The Lounge

Louisiana, 1948

Roy Kenner decided to give the raggedy neighborhood kids something to do by putting on a talent show in his spacious backyard. He was one of the fortunate few to own a house and land. That summer day he announced his niece Rosie would sing the cute jolly tune "The Very Thought of You" by Billie Holiday. The modest seventeen-year-old stepped out of her uncle's back door and onto his stage on the porch in a fitted cotton hand sewn red dress. It meticulously showed off curves she knew would demand attention when she entered the prime of her womanhood.

Most of the town sat on the grass of her uncle's shack. Shy Rosie could barely lift her head. She noticed the once talkative atmosphere had changed. Now she only heard silence along with a few whistles. When the flower in her hair began to slip, Rosie grabbed it delicately and held it in her hand while looking out into her shabby, country audience.

She was taken back. Rosie noticed how everyone stared at her in amazement. Some of the women even slapped their husbands, as their remarks weren't fit for children's ears. Her aunt had pressed out her long loose wavy hair, which she normally wore in a sweaty, messy ponytail. But now it hung halfway down her back like silk. Her pretty light-baked pecan skin tone glistened like fresh honey. The more the crowd gawked at her appearance, the more she felt unsettled to her stomach. She looked down at the heels her aunt let her borrow until she noticed Tyson leaning against an oak tree.

Mister Tyson Carmichael stood six feet three inches with a bold masculine stance and rock-hard muscles. His gorgeous smile revealed perfect teeth that glistened against his dark milk chocolate skin. Rosie adored his thick head of curly jet-black hair—compliments of Spaniard roots from generations back— the most. She loved him since she was fifteen years old. Tyson, her cousin Booker Kenner's best friend, came around like family. He was five years older than Rosie, and he never paid her any attention until today.

He looked stunned and tense like most of the men in the audience, only his mouth hung wide open. She giggled a little to herself as Tyson stood up straight in his signature manly stance, closing his mouth and holding onto his belt buckle like the World War II honorably discharged veteran he was. He poked out his chest a little more than normal and gave her a confident smile and a wink that she took as a cue to begin singing.

She turned her entire body in his direction and let out a ravishing, soulful bellow that made most of the audience jump. It seemed impossible that such a strong, controlled voice could come from such a quiet and timid girl, the one the small negro community considered doomed to a life of singleness because her head was always in the clouds. She had no potential of any real beauty to them, but it turned out that she was the most unappreciated extravagant swan in the entire area.

For the first time, everyone saw what her Aunt Mattie had always told her since she was small. She was stunning and flawless with nothing to be ashamed of. Aunt Mattie took care of her like her own daughter ever since Rosie's mother died mysteriously in her sleep when Rosie was too young to even remember her. Her father decided that it was best for Aunt Mattie and Uncle Roy to raise her.

Rosie held her note long enough to show off her range, singing runs until she was out of air. Then, she stood up straight and embraced possibility for the first time. She batted her eyes at Tyson seductively and then continued to sing the popular melody in a quieter tone that mimicked the original version. The neighborhood cheered her on with "go girl" and "sing it Rosie."

Tyson stood there enjoying the song he knew she prepared solely with him in mind. He didn't whistle like the others, and he didn't cheer. He remained in his manly stance expressionless, however, Rosie could feel he was captivated.

Tyson always considered Booker like a brother to him, which naturally made Rosie a humble, meek little sister. But today, he saw a woman for the first time. A woman he wanted to wake up to every morning. A woman he wanted to have and hold. A trustworthy woman he would be loyal to and have a tribe of children with.

When she finished, everyone stood up shouting and applauding. Her aunt waved and blew her an affectionate kiss. Uncle Roy quickly ran over and hugged her tighter than he ever had before. This made Mattie upset. She knew exactly what her husband was thinking, and she didn't want that for her niece. She always told Roy that Rosie could sing, but he never took it seriously. Now he was aware and filled with glee. Mattie new Roy was plotting and planning big plans in that moment.

Later that night after all the fun had died down and the country folk went back home, Rosie went toward the room she used to share with Booker before she got too big to share and Booker took the living room couch. As soon as she opened the door she saw a single white ranunculus on her bed with a note that read, *I thought you would like this. Tyson.*

***

Bounce Back From Tragedy

Roy started building an addition to their wooden shack and had all kinds of visitors come by to discuss plans, deals, and shows. Rosie could hear the disagreements between her aunt and uncle late at night. She didn't understand most of it, but her aunt repeatedly told Uncle Roy, "That's not the life my sister would want for her, and it's not the life I want for her either."

Tyson's visits had become more frequent after the talent show. Instead of hanging with Booker, he spent most of his time with Rosie. They took long walks up and down the dirt roads. She never knew she could feel so connected to another human being. It felt like they knew each other's thoughts the way they constantly finished each other's sentences.

One evening while walking by a nearby pond, he grabbed Rosie's hand for the first time. All kinds of happy emotions rushed through her body when he locked his hand with hers.

"Rosie," he said in a deep tone. He stepped in front of her and held her hand tightly.

"Yes Tyson?"

He moved his hand underneath her chin and inched closer to her lips, but Rosie flinched. Tyson frowned, cleared his throat, and released her hand.

"I'm sorry. I better get you home." They began to take the dusty pathway back toward her uncle's shack. They walked in silence with an unusual gap between them, and Tyson walked briskly a few steps ahead. Rosie admitted to herself that if she didn't make up for their missed moment, her relationship with

Tyson would be at risk, especially after loving him silently for so many years. She needed to be with him but was unsure of herself.

"Tyson," she whispered.

"Yes."

"Could you slow down?" He slowed his stride.

"Tyson," she repeated.

He took a deep breath before responding. "Yes, Rosie?"

"Can you just stop and look at me please?"

He stopped and looked at her without saying a word. She smiled. He wasn't as mad as she thought, but he looked irritated. "I'm ready now."

"No, you're not. I don't know what I was thinking. I'm not upset with you. It's okay."

He wasn't telling the truth. Although he wasn't mad, it was not okay. Rosie was eighteen now, and a lot of the girls in town were already married with their first child. He always treated her with respect and she knew their connection ran deeper than the ocean. They were in love and she wanted to become Mrs. Tyson Carmichael. She walked up to him and placed his hands around her waist. He brought her close into his embrace. She moved her lips toward him to let him know that she wasn't scared, and she was no longer a little girl. He pressed his full lips into hers. As he kissed her lips with pent-up passion, she kissed him back with an equal vigor. A moan sounded from his throat as she pushed her body closer to his.

59

Bounce Back From Tragedy

They still had some ways to go before they reached Rosie's home. Tyson pulled away because Rosie dare not let him think she wasn't all the way ready for future marriage. He placed his forehead on hers. Comfortable in his embrace, she held him tight.

"I love you Rosie," he said with honest sincerity.

"I love you too, Tyson."

Booker and Roy were heading to the next town from the opposite direction to gather supplies for the home addition. Booker spotted Rosie and Tyson first and stopped dead in his tracks.

"What's wrong with chu boy?" Roy looked ahead to see what had caught Booker's attention. His fatherly instinct kicked in right away and he clenched his fists, but Booker pulled at his arm before he could take a step.

"Pop, let's just leave them be. Rosie's a good girl and Tyson would never disrespect you or her."

"I don't like this," Roy admitted in his raspy voice. "He betta not mess things up for us."

"He's not pop. Now come on. He's over every day. He sure hasn't been coming to see me. You've just been too busy to notice, but Aunt Mattie likes the idea."

"Well, I'm watching now. Like a hawk!" They decided to turn around and take another route.

Uncle Roy eventually finished his addition. After Sunday dinner, he invited Rosie in for the first time to preview the place he knew he would groom her to become a superstar jazz diva. He often chuckled to himself, finding it hard to believe that so much unnoticed talent was right under his nose for so long. For months he demanded that she didn't open the former back door, which now led into his modest, but well put together juke joint. Uncle Roy covered her eyes with a blindfold and led her into the once forbidden area. He counted to three and removed the covering. She gasped at his hard work and precise design.

Her eyes scanned the room. She was speechless. She recognized a cluster of table and chairs to her immediate right from Mrs. Perley's old diner. They were old and worn but looked nice with a fresh coat of paint. On the wall to the left rested a bar area with open space in the middle of the room. The space felt cramped but good enough to serve its purpose as a dance floor. Rosie's eyes fixated on the stage straight ahead. It was nothing more than a simple one-step platform, but it had a microphone and a few seats for band players. Rosie walked slowly toward the stage. She stepped onto the platform and gripped the microphone in her hand. The biggest grin spread across her face. She was honored that she inspired Uncle Roy to build something so magnificent.

Rosie stepped down off the stage and twirled around.

Bounce Back From Tragedy

"So, what do you think sweetheart? You like it?"

"It's wonderful Uncle Roy. You're making history around here. You already have. The folks around here are going to love you even more than they already do."

"Well, Miss Rose, that's what we'll call ya," he said walking over to her. He placed his hands on her shoulders. "I built this for you, suga. You've got what it takes to be a name people will know and remember."

A cold shiver formed goosebumps on Rosie's arms. She didn't expect this. She was caught off guard. How could all of this be for her? She knew he was building a club, but she thought he would only allow her to sing from time to time if she begged and pleaded. Rosie never thought she would be the sole reason for months of his hard work and labor.

"I don't know Uncle Roy. I don't think that's such a good idea. Maybe you should find someone else."

"There is no one else. Honey, no one else has a voice like what you've got. You are an original, and because of you we are going to get out of Bucket, Louisiana."

"Well what did Aunt Mattie say? Up until the talent show she's the only one I let hear me sing. I don't want to upset her."

"Now listen, don't you worry about your Aunt Mattie. You want to obey your Uncle, don't you?" She nodded. "And you like singing. As a matter of fact, you love it right?" She nodded again. "Good! It's settled then."

She held up her hand to get her uncle's attention before he turned away.

"Uncle Roy?"

"Yes, Uncle Roy's star. What is it?"

"I was just wondering if you could talk to Tyson about it. I just want to know what he thinks."

"Tyson! What do I need to ask that pretty looking girl anything for?" He waited on a response from his niece, but she didn't look at him. She just stared at her hands.

"Yea I saw you two the other day. I thought you knew better than that, hmm!"

Her head shot straight up. She read her Uncle's face and knew exactly what he was referring to.

"You are classy. He's used to all them army girls that hang around the base. You are something rare. You have this look about 'cha and when you open your mouth to sing, no one would ever imagine the beauty and strength that comes out of ya."

Shrinking back, she tried to explain. "I know. It's just that he promised to take me to the city someday. Tyson said the world is out there for me to see and he's going to show me."

"Show you how?" Uncle Roy cocked his head to the side as his face turned up with disgust. "Show you how, gal?" Rosie put her head down and didn't respond. "I know Tyson. Known him since he was a boy. Now he didn't pay you any mind until he saw what you had. A gift! He ever tell you about that woman he's married to from the next town over that he never goes to see?"

A rush of panic traveled down Rosie's spine. Her chest tightened, and her breathing became shallow. "What do you mean Uncle Roy?" Surely, Uncle Roy was confused. Rosie knew everything about Tyson, and he knew everything about her. They fit perfectly together. This news just couldn't be true.

He shifted his head to the other side. "That girl he's married to. You know about her?"

Rosie's vision started to become hazy from tears forming in her eyes as she stood in silence searching for falsehood within Roy.

"Interesting how he gained such a liking to you after the talent show. After the show you put on... what young man wouldn't be desiring you? I've never heard so much buzz about one person in all my life. And the buzz is about you. How sensational you are! Tyson likes the way you look on his arm. He wants to be somebody. He's arrogant and hot tempered. That's how he ended up in all that trouble way back, and it's why his daddy made him enlist in the first place."

Rosie's legs began to tingle, and her mouth became dry. Tyson never mentioned any flings. He never said he was married.

"You gonna stick with your uncle, Miss Rose. Tyson ain't for you. He can't have my baby. You deserve better. All he's doing is filling your head with jumble with all these walks ya'll been takin' and such."

Suddenly they heard heavy footsteps coming their way. With a stream of tears rolling down her cheeks, she and Uncle Roy glanced at the door that led back into the house. Booker stood there with Tyson right behind him.

"What's wrong Ro?" Booker questioned. She turned her head the other way and folded her arms. Tyson walked past Booker and headed toward Rosie. He touched her face tenderly and turned her toward him while Uncle Roy stood their annoyed and angered. She yanked her head away and tried to move out of his grasp, but he held on to her and waited for an explanation.

"Ro, what's wrong my love?" he asked, his voice laced with concern and anxiousness.

"Are you married?" she asked with clutched teeth and fiery eyes.

Tyson raised his eyebrows. His heart sped up. He didn't know how to respond.

Her voice quivered as she repeated the question. "Are you married?"

He couldn't stand the pain that echoed in her voice. He didn't tell Rosie about her because he never wanted her to know. Besides, the feelings he had for his ex-wife didn't come close to how much he loved and adored Rosie. Although he knew her most of her life, he didn't pay attention to her until that special moment. But that wasn't why he loved her. The woman she was on the inside captivated him. She was smart and had good ideas. The ugly duckling was now the prettiest swan in the town. She had always been the most beautiful, but no one noticed because she was a quiet homebody. Now the word about her loveliness and appeal had spread around.

His grasp loosened, and Rosie backed away still waiting for an answer. Tyson glanced up at Roy and noticed the corner of his mouth curved upward with delight. He walked closer to Rosie, but words wouldn't come out. Tyson knew what this was truly about. From the moment he noticed the extra lumber and nails at the back of the house he knew Roy had set his mind on using Rosie's gift to make a profit. The only one who didn't realize it was Rosie, partly because of denial.

"I-I…" He wanted to explain his situation, but he couldn't find a way to make Rosie hear him. Marrying his ex-wife wasn't a good idea, but people put so much pressure on him, he thought he had to. He didn't love her. He spent so much time with her only to discover she was a cunning and malicious woman who didn't remain faithful. The love of his life was standing right in front of him. There was no way to make a half-truth sound good or decent. He should have told her before. He should have explained.

His face scrunched up with worry. He tried to reach for her hands, but she took another step back. The lump in his throat was hard as a rock. "I'm not married anymore Rosie. I shouldn't have ever married her." Tyson was afraid of what she'd think.

He couldn't risk shattering her fragile heart, and he didn't know what kind of horrible picture Roy had painted.

Rosie's body temperature began to climax as she waited for Tyson to finish explaining. However, he kept fumbling over words that didn't make sense. Her skin turned warm. The more he stalled, the more she knew that there was a whole lot Tyson was hiding. She began to slowly shake her head from side to side with a burning sensation radiating from her heart. Uncle Roy was right. Tyson really didn't care. He just wanted to be around the small-town prize, something to look good on his arm.

So many thoughts ran around her head, and Tyson's sudden stuttering problem insulted her. She put her hands up in complete frustration.

"Stop it!" She saw guilt and pain in his eyes. "Liar!" she screamed as she rushed past Tyson. She sobbed as she ran back into the house and slammed the door.

New York, 1961

The scent of freshly buffed floors filled the air. The diva of all divas entered through the grand staircase with a commanding strut. Her designer sparkling pumps tapped against the marble floor as she continued up the staircase into the main lobby.

"Right this way Miss Rose," the bellman instructed in his custom concierge red hat, jacket, and black slacks. He led her to a private dressing room at the luxurious New York Lounge. Only the greats dazzled and entertained in the hotel's showroom, which only welcomed elite patrons. She pardoned her manager, assistant, stylist, and the rest of her entourage to find some alone time and silence—the way she liked it before every show.

Rosie walked into her star-studded dressing room and closed the door gracefully behind her. Sweet treats and gifts covered the table, but she spotted her favorite right away. Bright bulb lights surrounded a beautiful boutique of white ranunculus next to the elongated mirror. Her absolute favorite flower. Only one person knew that. She received the flowers before every show, either in her dressing room or hand delivery. She hadn't received them in a while, not since the big blow up years ago.

Rosie was at the top of the list when it came to great jazz singers. She had already sung at the best clubs in the country and helped to break down barriers of racism by singing for all-white crowds time and time again. Tonight, was a special one. She was continuing her tour by putting on a performance that would linger in people's memory for years to come. Though confident, the butterflies in her stomach began to form. But, not because of the performance. She knew he was here in the same building, and he would demand they talk.

Rosie knew saying no wasn't an option. Although she had forgiven him for his original fault, their on-again-off-again relationship had lasted for over a decade. She knew Tyson would ask her to marry him, and this time he wouldn't take no for an answer. However right now, she had an eager crowd waiting, and she was going to put on a fantastic show.

Miss Rose took one final look in the mirror and fluffed her hair. She stood up in her snug spaghetti strap satin gown, stepped outside of the dressing room and headed toward the stage. It was time to perform, and he would just have to be patient and wait.

Mira Cassidy is an Indianapolis motivational speaker, journalist, and author. Mira found peace and serenity in writing at a young age. A love for the art form blossomed in 2015 when she returned to complete her degree after an eleven-year hiatus. After enrolling in additional English and creative writing courses, the depth of Mira's creativity was unlocked, and she produced her first short stories and poems.

Today, Mira is a very busy and devoted mother of three. She uses her voice to raise awareness on the pain and suffering caused by domestic violence and adverse childhood experiences. She also advocates for more funding and focus for area schools to service children who are exceptional learners. Mira firmly believes that anyone can bounce back from traumatic experiences with the right resources and support system, and she encourages others to heal and find inner peace.